Happy Parenting!

# When Mommy and Daddy Say

NO

# They Still Love You

## Nancy J. Ennis

### Illustrations by Cynthia Meadows

KIDS
BROWN BOOKS KIDS

This book is dedicated to all the Tot Town
families that I have had the absolute pleasure
of working with over the last thirty-two years.
You all have made me a better educator of
young children, and a better person in general.

*When Mommy and Daddy Say NO, They Still Love You*

Brown Books Kids
16250 Knoll Trail Drive, Suite 205
Dallas, Texas 75248
www.BrownBooksKids.com
(972) 381-0009

A New Era in Publishing™

ISBN 978-1-61254-198-3
LCCN 2014947906

Printed in the United States
10 9 8 7 6 5 4 3 2 1

For more information or to contact the author, please go to
www.WhenMommyAndDaddySayNO.com

# ACKNOWLEDGMENTS:

I want to acknowledge my family for all their love and support with this project: my partner, Cynthia Coleman, my mother, Mildred Ennis, my late father, John Ennis, my uncle, Don Ennis, and my aunt, Dottie Ennis. I love you all very much.

I also want to recognize two very amazing and hardworking women: Nicole Alvarado and Estella Vera. They are my assistant directors, my right and my left hands, and I appreciate all of their support and encouragement during the writing and publishing of this book.

Thank you to Milli Brown and the outstanding group of professionals at Brown Books Publishing Group.

When Mommy says **NO** about staying up past your bedtime, she says this because she wants you to get enough rest so that your mind and body will grow big and strong.

When Daddy says **NO** about playing with your ball in the street, he says this because he wants to keep you safe and away from harm.

When Mommy says **NO** more ice cream after you have had two scoops, she says this so you won't get a tummy ache.

When Daddy says **NO** jumping up and down in the car and sit in your seat, he says this because he is helping you follow the law and keep your body safe.

When Mommy says **NO** soda or candy for breakfast, she says this because she cares about your health and development.

8

When Daddy says **NO** he will not hang up your coat for you, he says this because you are a capable person and you need to have self-help skills to succeed in life.

When Mommy says **NO** you can't live at Grandma's house, she says this because she loves you and would miss you so much.

When Daddy says NO you can't eat pizza every night for dinner, he says this because it is important for your body to eat a variety of different foods (pizza once a week is OK).

When Mommy says **NO** you can't talk to strangers, she says this because the world can be scary sometimes and not all grown-ups are nice to children.

When Daddy says **NO** you can't run with food in your mouth, he says this because he doesn't want you to choke.

When Mommy says **NO** you can't climb on the roof of the house, she says this because she doesn't want you to get hurt and go to the hospital.

When Daddy says **NO** to hitting your baby sister, it's because he wants you and your sister to truly care about each other and be very good friends when you grow up.

When Mommy says NO you can't sleep in her bed, she is saying this because you have your own special bed, and you need to be independent.

16

When Daddy says **NO** you may not hit people, and that we only hit balls, he is teaching you not to hurt others.

When Mommy says **NO** because you want to play outside in the snow without a coat on, she says this because it is too cold, and it's her job to take care of you.

When Daddy says **NO** you can't cut your own hair, he says this because he doesn't want you to hurt yourself with sharp scissors.

19

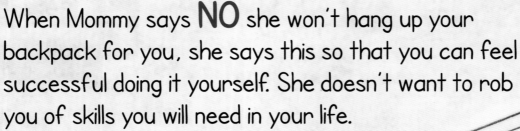

When Mommy says **NO** she won't hang up your backpack for you, she says this so that you can feel successful doing it yourself. She doesn't want to rob you of skills you will need in your life.

When Daddy says **NO** he won't carry you, he says that so you can walk with your own two legs and be independent.

When Mommy and Daddy say **NO**, they still love you.

# PARENTS:

Your job is to teach your children how the world works. Set limits, be consistent, and love them unconditionally.

The most important job in the entire world is being a parent. Guide your children so that they will grow up to make good choices. Their success depends on you. You are their security and most important role models.

So, please don't hesitate to tell your children NO. Your children's success and happiness depends on it.

# ABOUT THE AUTHOR

Nancy J. Ennis was born in Lawton, OK, but has lived all over, from Baltimore, MD, to Atlanta, GA, from Church Falls, VA, to Fort Leavenworth, KS. Her father was an Army officer, and he moved the family often. She graduated from Sacramento State University in 1982 with a BA in political science, and after graduation she began teaching children ages 2-5 at Tot Town Child Development Center, Inc., in Sacramento. She eventually bought the company with her partner, Cynthia Coleman, and has been the center's owner since 1993. Nancy currently lives in Gold River, CA, with Cynthia and their beloved beagle Hunter.

Tot Town's philosophy is to teach children independence and self-help skills, which in turn builds a child's confidence and self worth. Their motto is, "Don't do for a child what a child can do for themselves."

With this book, Nancy hopes to give parents the validation they need simply to say NO. Their children will still love them. In fact, they will respect and admire them more.

# ABOUT THE ILLUSTRATOR

Cynthia Meadows, a native Texan, draws and paints on anything she can find. Whether it is cartoons on the sides of her homework in elementary school, paintings as Christmas gifts, murals or faux finishes on walls, or illustrations and storyboards for advertising agencies, she has continually decorated the world. Cynthia's desire to look inside characters is the reason she loves to illustrate children's books, to create characters, and to give the reader a positive, often humorous, view of life.